# Ungone

First published in 2025
by Rough Trade Books

ISBN 978-1-914236-58-7

Design by Office Of Craig

Cover illustration adapted from *Studien in
der Anatomie des Nervensystems und des
Bindegewebes (Studies in the Anatomy
of the Nervous System and Connective
Tissue)* 1875, vol. 1, pl. 30, figs.1-5. Image
access courtesy of the National Library
of Medicine.

Printed and bound by Short Run Press Ltd

# Ungone

Hannah
Patterson

*Hannah Patterson*

ROUGH TRADE BOOKS

James Patterson

The idea, when it first occurred to me, seemed... audacious. Transgressive. And quite possibly ill-advised. Clever. But unformed. Yet... simple. As if it had been lying dormant, just waiting to be discovered. And developed, into...

A plan.

To explain...

I am Eve. I am 45 years old.

No, 46.

Wait, am I...?

Yes. 46. If that's necessary to know. If that's helpful—to define me. My mother is ill and on the demise. Or on the wane, as my brother likes to say, as if it makes it more palatable somehow.

To think of her as a candle, that's slowly snuffing out. She has dementia. And it's in its 'latter stages'. She has been in a home for nine months now. Ten, maybe. I'm not great with numbers, as you can probably tell. And I've been away—for work—for the last year. On a research secondment, in Antarctica. I am a scientist and academic. If that's helpful too, to know. I study snow, and ice. And glaciers that are breaking down.

During this time, my brother has been looking after her and overseeing the transition she's made to living in care. But over the course of the last year, he and his husband decided to move to Australia, with their two young children. Their twins. To Melbourne, where his Australian husband is from. They've had enough of England and want a better life for their IVF babies. So off it is to the land of opportunity and sun. Or is that California? Well, either way, who could blame him. They had picked *a* land of opportunity and sun, and were going to start a new life in it.

We were supposed to have a crossover week, my brother and I. After I returned and before he left. A week to say hello. To recalibrate and catch up. To transition and 'handover'. Then say goodbye again. But I got trapped in McMurdo. The weather there—well, everywhere now—is very unpredictable. So by the time I got back, he had gone.

He'd let himself into my flat and left a bottle of port as a welcome home. And a note—

*You'll need this to warm you up after all that snow and ice. Come visit.*
*It's a long way, I know, but still come. To warmer climes! We'll miss you.*
*Give Mum a kiss from me. Several, and often.*

Several, and often. The words upset me for some reason.
The cadence of them.

Next to the port, was a picture of him and his husband and
their two little identical, identikit offspring, who I barely knew.

So... he had gone. And it was all on me now. To visit. To sit.
It felt like a lot. A lot of pressure, and a lot of pain. Particularly
after months of putting this moment on ice.

*She probably won't recognise you,* he'd said, the last time we
communicated. *Prepare yourself for that. It's been a rapid decline.*
*And she doesn't contain the same properties. I've had time to adjust,*
he told me, *but for you, it will be much more of a shock.*

Well, good to know.

I was preparing to leave my flat, a couple of days later, preparing
to go and see her. For the first time. I was still a little groggy
from travel and acclimatising to being back. McMurdo was
intense and distancing from the outside world. Otherworldly.
Like the rest of humanity didn't exist. Even though we were
there explicitly to find ways to make its existence continue. It
had its own rhythms, and contact with anyone not there was

limited. It had felt like a time away from real life and real responsibility. Like time suspended. I'd never really experienced that so extremely before, and there was a reluctance in me to settle back into this old life, with its old habits and accountabilities.

I'd got everything ready, I thought, including a couple of books she liked, so I could read to her. A bunch of flowers. Daisies. Simple, but bright. Her favourite. And also myself. Her second favourite. I'd got myself ready too—emotionally I mean. At least I thought I had. Turns out, not so much. Because when I got to the front door, of my flat, I just couldn't face it. The prospect of it. Like everything was about to shift on its axis, and if I didn't go, it would stay as it was. So instead of going, I sat down on the hall floor, and lowered my forehead to the wood, and didn't move for a while. And then I opened the port.

The next day, I made it out of the flat, and got a cab—thinking that might help. I got it right up to the gates of the home but instead of getting out, when it slowed and stopped I asked the driver to turn round and take me back home. I'd got the wrong time, I said. Making an excuse.

He didn't seem to mind. In fact he gave me his number, and said—

*Call me if you still want to go. When it's the right time.*

*Thank you*, I replied. But I didn't call.

The next day, the same. And the next. And the next. Not going in. A week of it. Maybe more, probably. Eight days. Possibly ten. As I mentioned, I'm not good with numbers. Unless it's for work, that's different. For some reason, with work, the numbers stick. The density of different kinds of snow, for instance. Fresh falling, much less—50-100kg/m³. Refrozen, much more—500-550kg/m³. Or the fact that it only took one month for the 200 metre-thick, 1,255 sq-mile Larsen B ice shelf to disintegrate. But life numbers—ages, anniversaries, years when things happened, things that are supposed to be significant—don't stick at all.

Then one day when I tried, I made it out of the cab and up to the entrance. Spurred on, I suspect, by the intermittent, as yet unanswered messages from my brother, asking how she was. But before I could lift my hand to turn the handle, it started to shake. It was almost uncontrollable. As if it wasn't attached to me, or remotely governed by my will. Just a hand, shaking. I felt its aftershocks though, rippling through me, down my arm and into my chest and stomach, and I thrust it back into my pocket—embarrassed that anyone might see me so disassembled and out of control—turned away and left.

I went to sit in the nearby park. On the edge of a small, dilapidated fountain. With a coffee, from the man at the stand by the entrance. And took some breaths, to calm myself. I watched the walkers and the joggers. And the groups of school kids and students, laughing and shouting. And the parents watching their children playing. Sitting. Watching. Worrying. Being bored. Attention wandering. Wondering if this was what they'd really wanted, this life. Telling themselves it was. Of course. Some of them sure of it, no doubt. Each to their own.

One of the women who was there, was sitting alone on a bench. She had a parka on. Do I mean a parka? Maybe it was a puffer. Or a... duffel. I never really know the difference. Anyway, she was hugging it tight around her, almost as if she was getting strength from it, or some kind of emotional sustenance. As if it was protecting her. She was staring into middle distance, across the grass, at nothing in particular. But she was clearly thinking hard. Very hard. About something. Maybe it was something specific. Or maybe it was something more generic and universal that was occupying her. Either way, she had a weight about her.

Nearby, a boy—7 maybe, or 8—was sitting on the ground. Writing, or drawing, in a pad. Concentrating. Also very hard. She glanced over at him, occasionally, checking in. But he never once looked over at her. And then she'd go back to her middle-distance staring.

Something about her made me want to go and sit close by. As if I too might find some sustenance. Or strength. So I followed my urge—almost before I could even analyse or question it—and walked over.

There was space at the end of the bench, which I signalled to.

*Can I?*

*Course.* A brief smile as she moved her bag, nearer to her to create more room.

*Thanks.*

She was quickly back in her own thoughts then, after glancing over once again towards the boy. Who was still writing, or drawing. Very industrious. Immersed in his own little world. Attention utterly caught.

And I sipped my coffee—the one I'd bought from the little stand at the entrance to the park—and pretended to look at something on my phone. Self-conscious, all of a sudden. Feeling stupid that I'd been so quickly and intensely drawn to this woman on the bench. As if she might sense it.

Moments passed. Then after one of them, she sighed. A deep, heavy sigh. I'm not sure if she even knew she'd done it.

*Are you okay?* I asked.

She looked at me, blinking.

*That's a big question*, she said. *I mean, are you okay?*

I thought about it for a second, then—

*Yes,* I replied, casting my mind back to my uncontrollable
shaking hand moment, meaning *No.* Meaning *No, I'm not.
I feel like my whole world is shifting on its axis. And I don't know
what to do about it.* But what came out was... *Yes, I'm okay.*

*I'm fine, really,* she explained, as she turned towards me. *I just
lost my job. Two actually, on the same day. Which is a bummer, to say
the least.*

*Oh, I'm sorry.*

*It was a shitty job. Well one of them was. But still.*

*What were they?*

*Cleaning. That was the shitty one. Not the cleaning itself—I like things
to be clean—I mean the people I cleaned for. They were shitty. And dog
walking. I actually liked the dog walking, but the woman who owned
the business is closing it and moving back to Portugal. If I'd have had
the money I'd have bought it from her, but she sold it to a bigger company,
and they already had enough walkers of their own.*

*That's a shame.*

*It is. I'll miss them, those dogs. Looking after them. It was so easy to meet their needs. And make them happy. Much easier than the people I cleaned for. Their demands were endless. Big houses. Big needs.*

*I can imagine.*

And that's when the thought occurred to me. Quite suddenly. The audacious idea. The possible solution, to my problem. Maybe, I could just pay someone else, to go and sit with my mother. Maybe, I could pay someone else to be me.

--------

When she first mentioned it—when she first asked me— I thought she was joking. That this was some kind of prank. Or dare. And I nearly laughed in her face. Because it seemed like such a crazy idea. I mean, who in their right mind would suggest something like that? And who in their right mind would agree to something like that? Was she crazy? She didn't seem crazy. Not at all. But you can't judge by appearances. If there's one thing I've learnt in life, it's that. Books and covers. Covers and books. Often, they just don't match.

Also something about it felt wrong. Immoral, or... unethical. (I've never really understood the difference, to be honest). Deceptive. Dishonest. Cruel, even.

But... in the silence that followed—that sort of hung between us—almost immediately, I started thinking about the advantages. How I could benefit from this proposal. I mean, I needed the money, of course. But also it felt like an opportunity. An *opening up*. A beginning, maybe, of something. A chink of light in the grey, greying greyness of everything.

And then, as she sensed my interest, and started talking about how it could work—as she warmed to her theme—I was persuading myself into it. Telling myself I'd be a fool *not* to do it.

*I mean the people at the home don't even know me yet*, she said. *Haven't even seen my face.*

Telling myself I'd be a fool not to do it for Tom. As well as myself. For the both of us. We could do with some luck, couldn't we? And I wasn't doing any harm, not really. It was her own daughter asking, after all. It wasn't like I was conning anybody. Anybody who would get hurt, when they eventually found out. If they ever even did. What was wrong with that?

And actually if anything, I said to myself, warming to my own theme, I was being helpful. This woman—*Eve*, she introduced herself as, eventually, *Eve Monroe*—she needed me, it seemed. Her mother needed me. I mean I was the only person who could help, really. Maybe the best person.

*Okay.*

*Okay?*

*Yes.*

*Really?*

*Why not? I'd like to help. If I can. Why not.*

She looked at me, Eve, after I'd agreed. To take her offer of a job. This rather odd job. She looked at me, kind of incredulous, I think, that I'd said yes. Faltering for a moment, having a quick chat with herself, inside her own head, about whether she should have asked at all. Whether this was the moment for her to back out. To suddenly grin, and say—*Only joking. What a ridiculous idea. If only, eh? I mean, who hasn't thought about it.*

But no. She didn't. Instead, she said—

*Wow, that's... great.* And smiled.

Such a simple transaction, on the face of it. As if we'd just agreed to meet for a drink. Or catch a film together, at the local cinema. Or handed back a borrowed book. Or exchanged a tip on how to fix a leaking tap. Or... well anything really, other than this.

---------

That night Danny called me. There was annoyance in his voice as soon as I picked up. Which I shouldn't have done, looking back on it. But I wasn't thinking straight, a little high on my audacious idea, and my new recruit. And fortified, by port.

*Why haven't you been in yet? To see her?*

He'd just come off a call with the home, and one of the nurses had let slip about my absence.

Fuck.

*I've had some kind of bug,* I told him, thinking quickly and thickening my voice—the way you do when you're a child, and nothing's really wrong with you, you just don't fancy going to school. *There was no way I wanted to pass that round the home. I'd have never forgiven myself,* I said. *If someone had got ill because of me. Or her. Imagine.*

*Right,* he said. *That explains it… why didn't you say?*

*I didn't want to worry you. Not on the other side of the world. You've got enough on your plate.*

*You don't need to do that.*

I could hear his anger abating. His initial knee-jerk reaction that I wasn't doing what I should have been and honouring our pact.

*Well I did, so...*

*Sorry, I didn't mean to...* he apologised. *Jet lag.*

*Still?*

*Age. Alcohol. Babies.*

*That'll do it.*

*Yes.*

*So, how's it going?* I asked, riding the change of topic. *Right move?*

*Early days. But it's good to be... somewhere else. For all of us. I can tell that already. And it's hot. It's really very hot.*

*Lucky you,* I said.

*Your choice,* he replied. *To study ice.*

True. My choice. But sometimes when you make a choice you don't really think through all the implications.

---------

Her flat, where she suggested we meet, was very nice. I'd cleaned a lot of flats like this, in my time, but this was one of the nicer ones. All scented candles and blankets *with a hint of cashmere* draped over furniture. And dark wood. Stylish but cosy.

She looked me up and down, once we were inside, and I had settled Tom in an armchair with his books, and said—

*You should wear something of mine, when you go in.*

Then swiftly, as she realised I might think her words were rude (which I didn't), she added—

*They'll be familiar. To my mother. To Edith. They'll give the sense of me. The appearance of me.*

*Okay.*

We went upstairs and we looked though her wardrobe. She was a little embarrassed, I could tell. There were a lot of clothes. Well a lot compared to mine. I mean how did one person need this much stuff? This much pretty similar stuff.

*I like coats,* she said, with a justifying tone. Not that I'd made any kind of comment about it. *There's so much less commitment with a coat. You're putting something on that's very easy to take off, and discard. Harder to do that with other clothes. Once you're out. A skirt, say, or a shirt. Or a pair of trousers. You're stuck with them for the day. Once you've made that choice, you've committed. And people will make assumptions. More wiggle room with a coat. Even though it may seem heavier, it's lighter. Less permanence. To me, anyway.*

*I've never thought of it like that,* I said. Which I hadn't.

I only had one coat. So that option wasn't really there. Course that didn't mean I wouldn't like more. Should the opportunity arise. Less permanence sounded kind of pleasant. And lighter. And on a more practical note, my coat was often either too warm or not warm enough. Which was, frustrating.

We—well, she—picked a pair of trousers. Wide on the leg. A dark blue colour. Or maybe it was more of a navy. Was it navy? And then a top—a lighter shade of blue. I'd say peacock. She thought teal. Round at the neck. A little loose. And one of her coats. Like a trench, sort of. Down to my calves. Halfway down. With a belt that could be tied at the waist. And trainers. Pumps, more like. Her feet were a little smaller than mine so they were kind of tight. A little pinch at first. But I was used to that. Ill-fitting shoes.

I had a memory flash, to a similar pair I'd worn in gym class. A specific incident. The white canvas, with patches of blood seeping through the end. My teacher, Mrs Tyler—one of those good ones you can have, if you're lucky—approaching me after the session, asking to look at my feet. The toenails, that badly needed cutting, and had caused the blood. A frown of concern on her face. *Isn't there anyone that's taking care of you? At home?*

Good question...

Good question, Mrs Tyler. Define 'taking care'.

---------

She looked great in my clothes, Erin. Much better than me. Although we looked very similar, her skin had a glow. And it suited the particular shade of blue of the top—a kind of teal. Made her look translucent. Luminous. I liked plain clothes, mostly. With the odd splash of colour. But mainly plain. I don't like to draw attention to myself too much. It's easier that way. So many different people to try and please. Better to play it safe, and neutral.

And we looked about the same age. Though she was 37, she told me when I asked, and I was 45. No, 46. I'd got that wrong, when I told her my own and corrected myself. *I'm not good with ages,* I'd explained.

*Well you'd think we were the same age,* she said. *If you had to guess. You'd probably think we were around the same age. That's having children for you.*

*I suppose it is. Or genes, I guess.*

*And money. Having it. Not having it.*

I didn't know what to say to that.

So, I moved on. *I should tell you things. About her. My mother. My mum. I don't know why I keep calling her mother. I don't do that, not normally.*

*Keeps it more formal, I guess. Like a job.*

*Maybe.*

She nodded. She understood. *Boundaries can help.*

*I should tell you things about me. Our family. Things you might need to know. In case the nurses ask.*

*Okay.*

*So... where to start?*

---------

She asked if I wanted tea. *Tea?*

We were back in the kitchen now. With its kitchen island, and its kitchen utensils hanging in a line over the silver hob. This was a room that announced itself as a kitchen. All properly kitted out.

*I'm good.*

*Or coffee?*

*It's fine.*

*Or wine. God, let's have wine.*

*Okay,* I agreed. She clearly wanted some wine.

She went to her fridge and pulled out a bottle. A dark, emerald green colour. Condensation clinging to it. Crisp and expensive looking.

*Is this alright?*

She held it up.

I nodded. I didn't care. But Chablis was nice I knew that much.

*Something for Tom?* she asked.

*Tom?*

He shook his head.

*No, he's good,* I said.

*Okay. Well just ask, if you change your mind.*

She took down glasses from a cupboard. Delicate. Long-stemmed. Then plunged in the tip of the corkscrew and ground it in. A little inelegant, which surprised me. I was much better at that. When she tried to pull out the cork, she couldn't budge it.

*I'm useless with these things.* A slight reddening on her cheeks, as if she knew she should be better. Was embarrassed somehow.

*Here, let me.*

She handed it to me. And in one swift motion, I twisted and pulled.

*Impressive.*

*Years of waitressing at weddings. And funerals. Very useful for popping wine corks, and people managing.*

*I bet.*

I poured the pale yellow liquid into one of the delicate glasses.

Then handed her the glass and poured one for myself. As if this was my kitchen. And I was the one in charge. And this was my wine.

---------

She was kind, Erin. I could tell. Some people just have that in them. Kindness. Innate. Giving—for her—seemed effortless. For me, giving is an effort. I feel like I give at the expense of something. Something in myself. That I'm subsuming my needs to those of others. Prioritising theirs. Which leads to resentment and a quiet rage. And becomes a vicious cycle of subsuming, resenting, raging. Repeat. Subsuming, resenting, raging. Repeat.

Very tiring, to be honest.

For her though, giving only seemed to give her more. It didn't result in a lack, but an abundance. Giving and giving and giving and giving. Growing and growing and growing. Repeat. I could tell all that about her, even really early on.

*Are you sure he doesn't want anything?* I asked her, nodding at Tom.

*He's fine.*

*Are you sure, Tom?*

He shook his head.

*Really?*

He nodded.

*Doesn't he speak?* I whispered.

*No,* she replied.

*Oh, why not?*

*He just stopped one day.*

*Why?*

She shrugged.

*Well, when?*

*After his dad left.*

*I'm sorry. That's awful.*

*It's okay. You don't need to whisper,* she said. *He knows he's not speaking. It's not a secret. He'll talk when he wants to. He's always done things his own way. Haven't you, Tom?*

Another nod.

---------

I wondered as we talked and sipped—as Eve told me things about her life and her mother—what it was that was making her want to do this. Even though she was telling me things, I felt like she was telling me fact things, not emotion things. My mum was born in _____. My dad left when I was _____. I had a dog called _____. It died when I was _____. We grew up in _____. We moved when I was _____. I went to university in_____. I used to work at _____. Now I work at _____.

Lots of facts. Like a biography on the back of a book. Where I was left to read between the lines. To glean the effect things might have had on her. Was it simply selfishness, what she was doing? Like she just couldn't be bothered to visit her? To look after her? And care for her. Or was it something more? Had she done something to her, her mother, when she was a child? Or since? Something unforgiveable? Something she wanted to punish her for?

It wasn't my business, I suppose. But I was still curious. I mean if I was going to stand in for her, obviously I'd be curious. If I was going to in effect *be* her. Anything I could ascertain was going to help. Surely.

*So, as a glaciologist,* I asked, sticking to fact things, *what would I need to know? If someone asks.*

*I really don't think it's going to come up in the conversation.*

*Just some basics.*

*Honestly, when people ask what I do and I tell them that I'm a glaciologist, they tend not to ask anything else. Unless it's their field. Then they don't stop talking about it. Usually at you.*

*So how do you actually spend your time? When you're working?*

*I teach. I research. I write papers.*

*Do you enjoy it?*

She had to think about that.

*The work itself, yes. Some of the people involved not so much.*

*Why did you want to do it in the first place? To be a glaciologist?*

*Is this an interview? It feels like a—*

*I genuinely want to know.*

More thinking, then—

*Science. It organised my thoughts. They were a bit... scattershot.*

*That's a good description. I like that.*

*So I knew that I'd have to be a bit more in control. I'm not a natural doer. I have to make myself do.*

*I'm a born doer,* I said. Straightening the pile of books on the coffee table in front of me.

*I can tell.*

*And what was it like in Antarctica?*

Tom looked up at that, I noticed. Out of the corner of my eye.

*Cold,* she said. *Bright. Either light the whole time. Or very dark. Enigmatic.*

Much like you, I thought.

*Being there...* she said, *it's called ice time. That's what people say. Ice time.*

*I like that too.*

*So do I.*

Tom nodded in agreement.

--------

The first visit... I was on tenterhooks the whole time
she was there.

*How long should I stay?* she'd asked.

*Maybe an hour, at first. Just to test it out.*

*Okay.*

*I mean, she'll probably sleep for some of it. I think that's what happens.*

*Okay. And what if she says she doesn't know who I am?*

Good question. I'm trying to ignore that scenario.

*I don't think she will*, I said, trying to reassure her. *From what
Danny's told me. I don't think she will.*

*And what if one of the people in the home guesses something's wrong?*

*I don't think they will.*

*But what if...?*

*You can always call me. If you really need to. However, I think you're going
to have to use your initiative.*

*Huh. Not sure that was in the job description.*

Funny.

*Funny,* I said out loud.

*It helps.*

*What?*

*Humour.*

*With what?*

*Life. I find it helps.*

---------

I was a little on edge, going in. Butterflies, at first. A bit like I was about to sit an exam. And hadn't really done my revision as well as I should have. I always hated that feeling. Kind of... undermining. Undermining myself, I mean.

I stood outside the doors, of the home, watching the shapes of people moving about through the frosted glass windows. Figures in white, walking swiftly and with purpose, and others—patients I assumed—much slower, and stooped over. Eventually, I summoned some courage, opened and passed through the door.

There was a nurse on reception. Frowning. Preoccupied. She glanced up when I appeared. Clearly busy. Her head elsewhere. Thinking about a task she needed to complete. Many tasks, I imagine. She raised her eyebrows, not recognising me.

*Hi, I'm...* the name Eve didn't quite make it out. *I'm here to see my mother.*

*Her name?*

Yes, *her* name. Easier to say. Than my new, assumed one. *Edith. Edith Monroe.*

*Ah!* Her demeanour instantly changed and she abandoned her task-planning and moved around to the front of the desk. *We've been looking forward to greeting you. Very much.* She patted my arm. *But we heard you were ill. You couldn't come.*

Had I been ill? Eve hadn't mentioned that. Had she? Had I forgotten? What kind of ill had I been?

*Are you better? You look okay. Very well.*

*Yes. Thank you. It was just...*

*Something going round,* she interrupted. *Much safer, that you didn't come. Very selfless of you.*

I nodded in agreement. Relieved.

*Well, let me take you to her. You must be dying to see her. It's been a year, hasn't it? Almost a whole year. That's what your brother said.*

*Almost.*

*So long. Too long. For family. How is he?*

She showed me down a long corridor.

*Who?*

*Danny? He likes Australia?*

*Oh. Yes. I think so.*

*That's good. Still, we miss him. He was fun.*

Fun? Interesting. Not the impression Eve had given.

*But now,* she said, stopping outside a door, *we have you.*
No pressure.

And with a little flourish, she opened it.

*Mrs Monroe's room,* she announced. *Please go in,* she ushered
me through, when I hesitated.

Into a small room, which was surprisingly nice. With a view, over the park. Not the bit where Eve and I met, I quickly checked. No chance of anyone having seen that.

*Good?*

*Yes.*

*I think so. This poinsettia,* she pointed to a plant in the corner, with bright red leaves, *is from me.*

*It's... cheery.*

*Exactly. Cheery.*

She felt its leaves for a moment. Then—

*Sit, sit,* she pushed me down into a chair. *I'll find her,* she said, clearly excited by her mission, and disappeared.

Now alone, my eyes swept the room, taking in the personal touches. A couple of pictures on the wall. A landscape. A seascape. Greens and greys. The patchwork coverlet on the bed. Homemade maybe. Similar colours.

And... shit, a photograph of Eve. In the corner, on a table. With a man—her brother? I hadn't thought of that. Why hadn't we thought of that? *The Subterfuge of Pretending to Be Someone Else and How to Navigate It 101.*

I got up and went closer, inspecting it, then glancing at my reflection in the mirror above.

It's fine, I told myself. I could pass. In her clothes, it was fine.

Calm down, and sit down. Which I did.

Moments went by, accompanied by the unnaturally loud ticking of the clock by the bed. Then—

Movement suddenly, at the door. The nurse, reappearing. And with her, holding onto her arm, a woman in her 80s. Unsteady on her feet. Hair grey. Wearing black trousers and a bright green shirt that brought out her eyes. I'd seen pictures of her. Eve had shown me. But she looked a lot older in person. In this room. Real. Not just an idea.

*Here we are,* said the nurse, leading her towards me. *Look who's here to see you. It's Eve.*

Edith just stared at me.

*Hello. Mum.*

---------

*How did it go?*

We met in the park, at the same bench. I had a coffee waiting for her. From the man at the little stand.

*Well?* I was impatient to know. Unsure for a moment whether this has all been a giant mistake. Welcoming this person into my life. So easily, and intimately. What was I doing?

*Pretty well,* she said. *I mean, she didn't seem fazed. To see me, instead of you.*

*That's good.* I think.

*She was quite... affectionate.*

*Really?* That surprised me.

*Yes. She didn't say very much, she just wanted to hold my... I mean your... hand.*

Tears sprung in my eyes at that. I could feel them, hot and brimming. I couldn't hold them in.

She reached a hand over, but I (strategically maybe, I'll admit) lifted my coffee cup at the same time so she pulled it back.

*And the staff?* I took a gulp. *Are they good with her?*

*Very,* she nodded. *You picked a nice place.*

*I looked at the brochures. It was my brother who picked.*

And then I lost myself for a moment. Upset—or was it annoyed? Or hurt, maybe?—that our deception wasn't immediately discovered. That my mother hadn't immediately noticed and shouted out, THIS IS NOT MY DAUGHTER. Like Erin had thought she might. As if no one could so easily take my place. As if I wasn't so easily replaceable. That however far her dementia had gone, she would still know that someone wasn't me.

*Do you want to stop?* Erin asked.

*No,* I said, looking up at her. Shaking my head.

I didn't want to stop.

---------

The next time I went in, it was for longer. I was a bit less nervous, now that I'd actually met Edith and was starting to get a feel for her.

But I was aware I couldn't take anything for granted. I was still me, not the person I was supposed to be. And that could very easily slip out. Or show.

Edith was in the day room, apparently, with several other patients.

*Residents,* Nurse Myka corrected me, when I used that term. *We call them residents. This is their home now. Right, Terry?* Voice louder.

A male nurse who was nearby, banging the coffee machine, trying I assume, to make it work, looked up.

*Right, Myka. As always.*

*This is Mrs Monroe's daughter,* she said.

*Eve,* I used the name. For the first time out loud. Very strange. *Please, call me Eve.* And a little… thrilling.

*Eve,* Nurse Myka smiled. Pleased I think that I had so quickly moved to this easier intimacy. *This is Eve.*

*Hey,* he said, wiping his hand with a cloth then coming over to shake mine. *Welcome to the madhouse.*

*Terry,* Nurse Myka remonstrated, gently slapping his arm. *Don't say that.* But her eyes were playful.

*Go see for yourself,* he shrugged.

*Want me to look at it?* I offered, pointing towards the coffee machine. I could see the problem. It was the same make that they had at a care home where I sometimes did a deep clean, overnight. It got a lot of use by all the night-time staff—even though we weren't supposed to—and it frequently jammed.

*No, you're okay,* he said, *you need to have the knack. Which today I apparently don't.* He banged the side again.

*I don't mind,* I persisted.

Then went over, pulled the water tray just a little, wriggled it round, and rammed it back in. Lifting it up at a slight angle as I did.

*There you go,* I stepped back. *It should work now.*

*Right. Thanks.* He was clearly surprised. Exchanging a little glance with Nurse Myka, which I clocked.

Mmmmm. Not very visiting-child-of-dementia-parent, Eve-like-behaviour, I suspect.

*For that,* he said, *you get a cappuccino. Can't say it's the best, but—* another shrug. *Go see your mum. I'll find you.*

*I'll show you where,* Nurse Myka ushered me down the corridor. Then—*But you were so quick when you came. We didn't do a tour.*

*Shall we do it now?*

*Yes, good idea.*

*Excellent.*

Excellent. All going well so far.

*This,* she said, leading me further down a corridor away from Edith's room, *is the dining area. They can eat here, residents. Or in their room, it's up to them. Chefs are good. You can eat too. Together if you want to. That's nice. Birthdays. Christmas. Anytime. But best to warn, if you can.*

*Right.*

*It's not too expensive.*

We put our head in. There were a series of round tables. All empty.

*People tend to have their places. Edith, when she comes, sits there. That's what she likes.*

She pointed to a corner table.

*Back to the wall, to see the room,* she explained.

*Nice,* I said. Adding, *Sensible,* when I realised she was expecting me to comment.

*Some residents,* she said—*they can't be on the same table.*

*What happens?*

*War. Come on.*

Back out and up some steps into a glass-lined corridor stretching over the car park, which connected the two bits of the home.

*Out there,* she pointed outside to the back, *is the garden. With a pond. Fish and ducks. Nice. Good for fresh air. Very important. Look.*

I looked. It was nice.

Down some stairs, then—

*The dayroom.*

It was large. Open plan. With several levels. Or... zones, I guess you'd call them.

*Hairdresser comes once a week. In there.* She pointed to a little anteroom, with a glass door.

*And we have games and music in the afternoons and other things over there, like magic.*

She pointed to another zone down a little slope—for wheelchairs, I imagine.

*Great.*

*And here...* she gestured. *Is your mother.*

I followed her gaze to see Edith sitting in a high-backed chair to one side, two men in similar chairs nearby. One reading. One sleeping. But she was picking intently at the hem of her cardigan.

*Eve is back,* Nurse Myka said loudly.

Then to me. *I'll leave you. Lots of work.*

*Of course. Thank you.*

I knew what that was like—generally having lots of shit to get done and rarely enough time.

*Hello.* I pulled up a chair, and sat down next to Edith. She didn't look up. Whatever it was about that hem was intensely involving.

I tried again. *Hello, I—*

*There you are.* I looked up to see Terry, with my cappuccino.

*Hope it's not gone cold*, he said, handing it to me.

*No,* I said. *I'm sure it hasn't. Thank you.* Taking it.

*Hello Mrs Monroe.* Voice warm. Enthusiastic. *How you doing?*

She sort of shrugged and peered over at my coffee.

*Wanting one too, are you? Course you are. And why not? Well now
your daughter here has cleverly fixed our machine, you can. Go on then,
I'll be back.*

She looked at me, then back down to her hem.

Okay, I thought. This might take a bit of time. Our... bonding.
And I took a sip. Of the cappuccino. Thinking about what to say.

*Not bad.*

Edith looked up, at the coffee, eyeing it.

*Want some of this one?*

She nodded, and I held it out to her.

She took a sip, and grinned.

*Not bad.*

There we go.

---------

It was weird going back into work that first day. I could feel the tethering happening. The feeling of restriction. Of the walls closing in. As soon as I passed through the doors.

*Oh hi, Eve. How was the Ice?* That's the pet name for McMurdo. Well some people's. Usually people that haven't actually been.

*Pretty... incredible.*

*Great.* Not that interested clearly. No follow-up questions. Or jealous, perhaps, that she hadn't been herself. This was Yvette, by the way. A colleague.

*How's your mum? It must have been a relief—to finally get back and see her.*

*Yes.*

*Quite a big decision, leaving her alone like that.*

And what business is it of yours?

*Well my brother was here, so...*

And actually come to think of it, how do you even know anything about my mum?

*Oh right, I see. Well that's good.*

*Yes,* I said firmly. *She's okay.*

*I just wanted to say something,* she came closer, *because I know people don't tend to. And it seems odd. Not acknowledging it. I mean, it's difficult isn't it? The responsibility.*

*It can be.*

*But you don't want it to define you, do you?*

*Um, no.* Hence why I've not really been talking to people about it.

*I just wanted to say, I know what it's like.*

*That's nice. Of you, I mean.*

*I just wanted to say I'm here, you know. If you want to talk.*

I wanted to say, *Could you stop saying I just wanted to say.* But I didn't, I said—

*Thank you. That's very sweet of you.*

*The thing is, when my mum died—*

*She's not dead.*

*Yes, it was a few years ago, sadly, I—*

*Mine.*

*Oh. No, I know, but it can be as if they are dead.*

*Well she's not.*

*Well...* I felt a change of tack coming, as she realised this line of questioning wasn't going so brilliantly. *There's been some stuff going on, since you've been away.*

*Stuff?*

*Here.*

I was clearly going to have to drag this out of her.

*Such as...?*

*Raoul has been promoted.*

*Raoul?* Figures. *Since when?*

*Last month.*

And why am I only just hearing about this now?

*How come?*

*Sonny resigned.*

*Resigned?*

*Read...* she looked around and lowered her voice... *was... let go.*

*Why?*

*Bit of a mystery. But he had to go straightaway, and we know what that means.* She put her finger to her nose and tapped it a couple of times. *He always did have a wandering hand.*

I really hate it when people say that. It makes it sound so... unimportant and benign. As if the hand had accidentally found itself there, after losing its sense of direction. As if there was no intention behind that hand. Whatsoever. No drive.

*No smoke without fire*, she said. *So now, Raoul.*

I'm not mad on Raoul I have to say. He's one of those slightly mediocre academics that seems to have got very far for no discernibly obvious reason. Just good at playing the game maybe. Picking a topic and sticking with it. Becoming the expert. Ploughing the same furrow. But he doesn't have 'wandering hands'.

*I mean it's temporary*, she said. *He's covering for now. Until they advertise. I assume you'll go for it?*

*Me? No.*

*Why not?*

Why not?

*All that responsibility. For what?*

*Recognition. More money.*

*More admin. More bureaucracy.*

*I always thought you liked responsibility.*

I'm starting to rethink that.

*It's what you give off,* she said. *But maybe, I figured you wrong.*

Maybe.

---------

Obviously I couldn't go in to the home all the time during the day, otherwise the nurses would be suspicious and wonder why I wasn't at work.

It was a delicate balance.

So I quickly found some new cleaning jobs, to make up the hours.

One was close by, which was handy. And the timings worked well. It was a family. A mum and a dad. Pretty conventional. And three kids. All under 8, by my reckoning. So I knew I'd inevitably end up being asked to look after them. *Could you just watch the children?* Another not in the job description, but it always happened. Literally every single time. Just wait...

*Do you live near here?* she asked. The first time I went to the house to meet her. A question which made me laugh, inside. Because how would I be able to afford to live near here?

*My mum's in a home,* I said, *just round the corner.*

*Which one?*

*Fairview?*

*Oh,* she said. *Nice.* She hadn't expected that. Covers and books...

*So it means I'm close.*

*That must help—with visiting.*

*It does. It means I can just pop in and out.*

*Handy.*

*Yes.*

*Well I have to say your references are amazing.*

*Thanks.*

*You must be very... in demand.*

*I don't know about that.*

*Lucky me.*

I just smiled, and shrugged.

*It's kind of crazy, really,* she said, *when you think about the people we all just let into our house, willy nilly, without thinking about it.*

I didn't, but hey. *I suppose it is,* I agreed.

*So... anyway...* She seemed a bit distracted. Like she had stuff on her mind. *Shall I show you around?*

*Great.*

*Show you what needs doing. Ideally, I mean, with the time you have.*

*Never enough.*

*No, I'm sure.*

*But you can show me what to... prioritise.*

*Exactly.*

And then her phone rang.

*Oh, excuse me... I need to...* She made a 'taking call' gesture. *It's work...*

*No please. It's fine.* This is my work too, actually.

*Oh could you just keep an eye on...* She nodded to the baby sitting in the high chair. *While I deal with this?*

See?

*No problem.*

No problem.

---------

*Congratulations.*

*It's temporary.*

*Even so.*

*Thank you.*

Raoul was enjoying his new office, I could tell. He'd already put a picture of his parents on the desk. And his child. And a couple of plants. And his PhD certificate on the wall. So it wasn't looking that temporary.

*So, where are we at?*

*With?* I hate it when people say 'we' when what they mean is 'you'. Where are *you* at?

*Everything*, he said. Helpfully narrowing it down. *You weren't the most communicative person while you were away.*

*It's very tricky there. The internet. Everyone has to share. And it's small. The capacity.*

*Still. You know how demanding the students can be.*

*I do.*

*Or should I say...* two sets of fingers lifted, in imagined quotation marks... *clients.*

*Hah.*

*Very entitled.*

*I suppose they are paying a lot.*

*Which means they certainly don't understand small bandwidths.*

*Right.*

This wasn't going very well.

*Have you worked out your paper?* he asked. Getting more specific now. *For the conference? I imagine you'll be presenting your findings?*

*... Yes.*

I actually had no clue what I was going to present at the forthcoming conference. Had not put my mind to it at all. Not one iota. But I couldn't tell him that. My new, temporary, boss.

*And to summarise...?*

*Well the ice caps are officially melting.*

*Yes*—dryly, deliberately ignoring the joke—*this we know. You didn't need to fly over 15,000 kilometres to work that out. And thus compounding the problem.*

Oh fuck off, Raoul.

---------

Pretty soon, I started to look forward to my visits. The staff in the care home treated me with respect. A respect I didn't command in my other life. They assumed I was wealthy—well, wealthier than them, or my real self, at any rate—which was weird to experience. Strange at first. The feeling of entitlement. Like I didn't realise it was me they were talking to sometimes. Me as Eve. Because people didn't tend to talk to me like that. Kind of... deferential.

*Can I get you a cup of tea?* they'd say. Or... *how are you finding her?* Kind of solicitous. I wasn't used to that.

I was super polite, always. Interested, in them, and their lives. (Which I genuinely was). I remembered their names. Every single one. Myka and Terry, of course. I saw them the most. But also Claire, who was a much newer and less experienced nurse, I discovered. And very... skittish, I'd say is the word. Roman, who seemed to do a bit of everything and often came round with the trolley. Magda, who came in to do hairdressing sessions. Mike and Pauline, two of the chefs. And Beatriz and Ariadne, two of the cleaners. And I remembered where they lived. And how long they'd worked here. And what their interests were. And their favourite TV programmes. And what it was like, cleaning in a home.

And after a while I even started to take them little gifts. A bar of chocolate. Or a piece of fruit. Or a tiny candle. Nothing fancy, but still. The sort of thing Eve might do, I imagined. I put thought into it. And I enjoyed the pleasure they got from it. The acknowledgement, of their work. And I always made sure the gift was suitable. Appropriate for who they were. Their tastes. Did they drink or not? What colour did they like? It always amazes me how many people buy gifts that they would really like themselves rather than for the person it's for. I mean, what's all that about? And I took the time to find out if their own parents were still alive. Or if they had any children. And what *their* names were. I suspected that this didn't happen often.

But most of all I enjoyed spending time with Edith. Her sense of humour, surprisingly impish at times, was infectious. With no history between us, every day I was there felt fun and fresh. I mean I had responsibility, sure. I was super aware of that, don't get me wrong. But it wasn't... weighted. I enjoyed giving my time to her. Reading to her. Plaiting her hair after it had had a wash. Sitting nearby while she drifted off, holding her hand sometimes. So she knew someone was close. Seeing her eyes open and search the room. Anxious at first, then reassured, on finding my face.

And I didn't get bored, which I'd thought I might, when I was used to so much physical activity usually. Plus it gave me time to read, which was a luxury you couldn't afford when there was so much cleaning to be done.

One of the first books I read to Edith, I found in the home, and it was the title that caught my eye. *Hot Milk*. It intrigued me immediately.

What did it mean?

*Hot Milk.*

It sounded so... dangerous. And alive.

I read it to her very quickly, in one sitting. And she was unusually still throughout.

And actually once I'd finished the book I wasn't sure I was any the wiser about the title. Milk as in mother's milk? Hot as in not good maybe? Not the kind of milk that's right for a child? Milk should be warm for a child. Is that what she meant? Not hot. That could burn. I looked it up, online, but I couldn't see any explanations anywhere. So I guess, it was open to interpretation. That was probably the point. There were lots of reviews and comments from people speculating. *Hot mess* maybe was that what it was invoking? That the main character was a hot mess. Also, some people pointed out, she was a barista and spent time making milk hot. Which seemed a little too literal, but not an unfair point. At least I assumed she was meant to be the main character because it was told from her point of view. Although that didn't necessarily mean that was true of course.

Anyway, it was pretty electric when I read it. The response I had. Maybe it was the timing. It felt kind of appropriate. This book about mothers and daughters. Parents and children. And who was responsible for who. And tricky illnesses, the ones you can't really see, which... resonated.

I read it again over a glass of red—or two—in the little local wine bar I'd found, close by to the home. Which I frequented on occasion, when I was wearing Eve's clothes. Then I saw another book by the same author and I read that to her too. And she seemed to love that just as much. And then I realised it was the last of a trilogy. About the author's own life. A 'representation' of her own life. And there was a book that came before that one,

and one before that. So we'd consumed them in the wrong order.
Backwards rather than forwards. It was kind of interesting doing
that, rather than in the order they'd been written. Having a
knowledge of who someone would become, when they didn't yet
know it themselves. The choices they'd make.

She lived in a world so unlike my own this author, and yet...
and yet here I was finding myself in everything.

These fractured women.

I mentioned her to Eve. *Oh god, yes, she's brilliant*, she said,
unloading the dishwasher. It sort of annoyed me a bit.
The ease with which she said it. Like of course I should
know. Effortlessly, just know.

Not like her actually. She wasn't one to put a person down.
Or make them feel small. Kind of careless.

---------

Pretty soon, I started to enjoy the days that Erin was visiting
my mother. On a practical level, it lifted a weight off me.
I didn't have to schedule it in, and try to stem my irritations,
or my anger, or my grief, or my sense of loss, or frustration,
or powerlessness. And hurt. All the complex emotions that
come with the ties of familial relationships that are tugging and
snagging and knotting and unravelling. All the resentment that

there was no point feeling, when the person responsible wasn't even cognisant of the effect they'd had on you and your life, or all the little fissures and damages they'd caused. Not that they'd done anything dreadful, you understand. But it all added up.

And then, on another, entirely unexpected and rather welcome existential note, it felt as if I wasn't quite me anymore. Someone else was busy being me, so I was free to be whoever I wanted to be.

The possibilities it opened up were endless. Glorious. And freeing.

Scary too. Who was this person? I felt a simultaneous rush of fear and elation. Like that feeling of falling in love. Pure, unadulterated pleasure and excitement, and utter terror all at the same time. The moment at the edge of a precipice, when you can either step back and go about your normal business or take the leap.

Is this how people felt who changed their name, I wondered? Who left, quite suddenly, in the middle of the night, and became... someone else. The person they were meant to be all along. I wasn't that person. I was dependable and steadfast. I subsumed my needs for those of others. I'd never leave. But look what I was doing now? It was out of character for sure. The character I'd been labelled with. But had it always been there in me, that possibility? A part of my character as yet unfulfilled or

fully realised, that was ready for change. Whatever that may be.
A casting off. Casting off my usual role. Casting against type.

Yes! I was going to try casting myself against type. That was now
my mission.

I wrote a list:

First, when I wanted to say no—when what I usually said instead
was yes—I was actually going to say no. *No, I don't fancy it, but
thanks.* No excuse. No pretending there was something else I had
to do. Just—*No, I don't fancy it, but thanks.* Why was that so hard to
say? My god...

Second, I was going to try new things. Things I had no aptitude
for. And not care that I had no aptitude for them.

And third, I was going to stop comparing myself to other people.

--------

There was one incident early on which freaked me out a bit.
It was a Sunday. Edith had been sleeping, in her chair in her
room, and I was reading—*Mrs Dalloway,* on this occasion. I'd
borrowed it from Eve, who'd said it was one of her mother's
favourites, and—

*She might like to hear it, don't you think? Read out loud.*

I'd been reading it out loud (as I'd been doing with all the books for a quite a while now) and Edith had fallen asleep. But I was deep in it so I kept on going. Unable to help myself. And I'd made a note of where we'd got to, when she closed her eyes. So we could go back to that exact spot, later. I was thinking about the heroine and her life choices, and her insistence on giving a good party, despite her obvious mental health issues that needed dealing with, when gradually, I became aware of a change in the room. A shift. The atmosphere more electric, suddenly, than it had been. Charged. I looked up to find Edith's stare, hard on me. Boring in. Untold depths in those black-flecked, emerald green eyes.

*I don't know you,* she said—the very thing we'd feared that hadn't happened at first but now was. Those eyes flashing. Accusing. I opened my mouth, unsure what to say exactly, just preparing to say something—anything—that might deflect, or distract, when—

The door opened and in came Nurse Myka—with lunch. *Here we have it.* Cheerful as always. With her cod and tartare sauce, and her spotted dick and custard.

She expected to get more of a reaction, given she had food, but Edith wasn't paying her any attention.

*I don't know you*, Edith said again. Eyes still boring.

How true, I thought, you don't. You absolutely don't. But I was a little hurt, I'll admit, because I thought we'd been getting on really very well, under the circumstances.

*I don't know her,* she turned to Nurse Myka, who was moving my bag—Eve's bag—so she could put the tray down. *Who is she?* Those eyes, back on me. *Who are you? WHO?*

I held my breath. Stomach churning. Mouth dry. I felt exposed all of a sudden. Like the imposter I was.

*Now come Mrs Monroe,* Nurse Myka said softly. *Come on.* A gentle reprimand. *It's Eve.* As she busied herself, moving plates onto the little table. *You know Eve. Don't you? Of course you do. She's your daughter. Wonderful daughter. The best. She comes here all hours to see you. Every day almost, if she can. Who does that, mmm? Who? Not many.* Knife and fork clanking onto the tray. *You're lucky, Mrs Monroe. Lucky, lucky, lucky.*

*Here, try some.* She held a piece of cod up on a fork, and Edith slowly took it in her mouth and started to chew.

*Don't worry,* Nurse Myka whispered over at me, loudly. Clearly the look on my face betrayed how flustered I was feeling. *Nothing to worry about. Not personal. Just hard she doesn't know you. Always hard.*

I could feel my cheeks were red. Red with Guilt and Shame.

*I mean what I say.* She gave her another mouthful. *You're very good with her. Very, very good. Other people's children—the children that come—soon as they arrive they're looking at their phones or their machines. Thinking about going, soon as they come. Giving excuses. Always. Wanting not to be judged—by me. I see it. I don't blame. We've all got reasons.*

I almost confessed to her then. I don't know why. She was very perceptive, Nurse Myka. I'd have to be careful with her.

*We shouldn't talk about my mother,* I said, *as if she's not here.*

---------

And so we continued. Weeks of Erin visiting. And me, when I wasn't at work, just trying things out.

Small things at first. Testing the water.

*No don't buy that—that's what you always buy,* I'd say to myself, in the supermarket. *Try that instead.*

Or... *why not pull out that dress that you bought and never wear. Which you knew you'd never wear when you bought it. But bought it anyway. Because you thought you might be the kind of person that wears that dress if you actually put it on and went out in it.*

Or... *why not this book, instead of that one. Or this film, instead of that.*

*Or this new pastime. This hobby. This class. This road. This bus. This—*

---------

*What do you do?* I asked Eve one day. *What do you do, when I'm with Edith? And you're not at work?*

She thought about it for a moment, then—

*I free myself.*

*What do you mean?*

*I go and do things that I usually wouldn't. I go and do things that people spent my whole life telling me I'm not very good at, that I have no aptitude for, that I should leave to other people. And I don't care. That I'm not good at them. I just do them anyway, because I want to, not because I'm going to be good at them. Or get better at them. Or better than someone else. Or the best. I just do them because I want to.*

*Like what?* I asked, intrigued by this idea.

*Well, yesterday,* she gives me an example, *I went on a big wheel.*

*At a circus?*

*More like a funfair. It was in a park near work.*

*Go on.*

*When I was young everyone used to tell me I was scared of heights. After I'd had a meltdown when the wheel got stuck for hours at the top, and I thought I was going to die. Quite reasonably, probably, looking back on it.*

*I'd say.*

*But yesterday when I got to the top, I wasn't scared at all, I was exhilarated. And as soon as I got down to the ground, I bought another ticket and went straight back on. Think of all the years I've wasted, not going on the big wheel. Because of what other people told me.*

I thought this was ingenious. An ingenious way to spend one's time. And I loved knowing it. And I enjoyed thinking about it. Thinking of Eve doing all the things she'd wanted to.

*What else?*

*On Saturday I swam naked.*

*In a pool?*

*A river. There was no one there. So I didn't bother putting on my costume. I didn't think I'd do that.*

*How was it?*

*Thrilling. Sort of... subversive. I was always told to wear a costume.*

*We never did,* I said. *We always swam naked.*

*Well those were our rules.*

It became a little game between us, when we caught up at the end of the week.

*Who were you today?* I'd ask, taking one of her bottles of Chablis from the fridge. *I hope you haven't run out already? Of other people to be?*

*Oh no,* she said, pulling the cork out like I'd taught her. *There are multiple, myriad versions of who I could be. It's endless. I'm starting to see that now.*

---------

For Edith's birthday we made cake. Well Erin did. Tom helping.

*Take pictures,* I said, *so I can send them to Danny. But be careful not to have any with you in.*

*I'm always careful,* she pointed out. *I've already told Nurse Myka that I hate to have my picture taken. That I think it steals my soul.*

*Clever.*

*I do actually. I think it's a control thing.*

*I get that.*

*But she clearly thought I was a lunatic.*

Then afterwards, when she came back to pick Tom up, bringing some of the cake with her—

*She said I had to be in these pictures. Because it was her birthday, after all. She got very insistent about it.*

*So what did you do?*

*First I took one of the two of them. Look.*

She showed me a picture of Nurse Myka beaming, standing next to Edith. Her poinsettia reaching out behind them.

*Nice.*

*And then I pretended that my phone died.*

*Sneaky.*

*Well, it worked.*

I sent the picture to Danny.

*Since when did you make cake? ;)* he messaged me.

*Who knew?* I messaged back. You'd barely recognise me.

---------

Spending so much time with someone else's mother inevitably led me to think about my relationship with my own. I'd loved her, so very, very much, but she'd never really known how to be a parent. She'd never protected me. Not properly. She didn't have it in her, most of the time. Probably because she was spending so much time trying to look after herself. Which I understood. Now, and then. But she had tried. She had tried to be a better version of herself.

When she died it was left to me, as the only child, to go and clear her flat. It was filled with books. She loved reading. And the range was huge. Something for when she felt depressed. Crime, usually, for that. Or a Mills and Boon. Nothing too challenging. Stories that sucked you in and took your mind somewhere else. Away from yourself. And then the opposite. The ones that made you think. Freud. Jung. de Bono. And always a book she'd recommend to everyone when she was at her uppest—that excited her greatly. That everyone she knew had to read because it was so mind-altering and life-changingly IMPORTANT.

One section—perhaps the most revealing, I realised, as I packed them altogether in a box—were the self-help books. A good forty of them, here or there. *Spiritual Alchemy. The Power of Now. Practicing the Power of Now. The Dance of Deception. The Dance of Intimacy. The Dance of Anger. Healing Sounds. The Feeling Buddha. The Invisible Way. Going on Being. Learning How to Learn. Sunbathing in the Rain. How to Save Your Own Life. Being Happy!* I could go on... lots of them were second hand from second-hand bookshops and I thought of the long line of women who'd diligently—or desperately—read them all, then offloaded them for some other woman to seek out. Self-help. Self-help. Shelf-help.

So she had tried. Here was the overwhelming evidence. She'd spent a great deal of her time trying. And trying. And trying. And failing. And trying. And failing. And falling. On and on. Because being in the middle is never enough it seems. Neither trying too hard, nor failing too much. Just being. I mean there'd be no failing really, if you didn't keep trying too hard. How peaceful that would be. Would have been, for her. I wish I could have helped her more with that.

I took pictures of the books in the box with my phone, then gave them to the charity shop. It's the thing I regret the most—letting that box go. Evidence, of all the lives she'd tried to live. All the better versions. It felt like a betrayal.

---------

Eve thinks I don't know. What they cooked up between them, these two women. They think I have no idea, that the person who's been sitting next to me these last months is a total stranger. And not in fact, my own daughter. If she did—think that I knew—she wouldn't have done it. She wouldn't have had the guts. She would have felt my judgement too keenly to have proceeded. With her *audacious*, half-baked plan.

Conscience is the inner voice that warns us somebody may be looking. I read that somewhere. And I think it's true. Conscience is the inner voice that warns us somebody may be looking. And that person that's been looking is me.

Yes, Eve, I see you.

And I mean, how *could* you? How could you do this, to *me*? Who weaned you, watered you, fed you, clothed you. *Made* you. Who sacrificed for you. Burying dreams and desires and opportunities and what-ifs, to prioritise your needs. You think this is how to treat me? *Me*?

How very... ungrateful.

It's not how your brother would behave. He left to start a better life, for his family, not to just suit himself. I mean I would have preferred that he didn't go. Of course. But I understand why. I'm not going to take it as a slight. A reflection of me, or our relationship. He's been a pretty easy son to have, all being said.

We've got on well. Very well at times. When he came out, for example. I think I handled that with considerable aplomb. I understood. What it took. And I knew how important it was, in that moment, my reaction. But you, Eve—

Neither one thing nor the other. Never emphatic enough. Never quite living up to expectations. Never excelling. Always holding something back. Going off on your little research trips. Half a foot in this, half in the other. I almost wish you'd rebelled. Got yourself some tattoos. Or a nipple-piercing. It would have been more interesting. Even if I didn't agree.

---------

One morning, when I was attempting, with limited success, to tackle my conference paper, I heard an actor on the radio. I don't know who, I didn't catch the name. She was talking about how playing a certain kind of character had temporarily affected her in her real life. Which caught my attention.

The part, she said, was that of someone very bullish. A canny negotiator. Who was used to getting their own way. Not her natural way of being at all, the actor. She was much more accommodating. Meeker. More... passive. Not so used to asking for what she wanted. Let alone demanding it. And at the time she was playing that character she had to negotiate something. A house sale, I think it was. I can't quite remember—I was in and out. It was something pretty big though. Something that would usually make her very uncomfortable. Give her anxiety. But, emboldened by the characteristics of the person she was temporarily inhabiting—imbued with her spirit and her verve—she behaved in a completely different way during her negotiations. She conjured her up in the day, just as she did on stage every evening. And noticed how very differently she was treated as a result. And how very different the result was.

It was quite a revelation. And really struck a nerve with me, I noticed.

Maybe this was what I should be trying to do in my professional life. Take on the attributes of someone else. Someone who could help manifest the work I wanted to be doing, rather than the work I actually was.

Yes.

And I looked down at what I'd written so far, for my paper. And I decided to start again.

To use this opportunity. To experiment. Explore. And write what I really wanted to write.

It was a new departure for me. More multi-disciplinary than any of my previous work. More philosophical. And psychological.

Why is it, for instance, that we can't accept the concept that the glaciers are melting? Six times faster than they were forty years ago. Losing 267 gigatonnes (Gt) of ice per year. That's a lot of their properties. And relating it to our inability to accept the nature of our own demise, and those around us. The ceasing to exist. As if the glaciers were in some way a mirror of our own selves. Our inability to accept their fate, an inability to accept our own.

Once I'd finished, I was pleased with the work I'd done. I felt that it reflected all the time and space and different outlooks I'd been accruing since I returned from McMurdo. All these different versions of myself that I'd been trying out. And trying on. Finally, I was finding a way to put them into my work, and make it mine. Uniquely mine.

I was excited. Emboldened.

*Well that was... interesting,* Raoul said to me, after I'd given the paper, and we were walking to the canteen.

*Thank you.* Joking—*I think...?*

*Unusual,* he said. Not joking. *A new direction?*

*Yes. It's good to try something new, don't you think?*

*It can be.*

*It's too easy to get stuck in the same old assumptions and hypotheses.* Try him at his own game, I thought.

*Still*, he said. Not playing. *Would have been good to have had a heads up.*

*How do you mean?*

*A warning.*

*Oh, I didn't realise that was necessary.*

*What you do reflects on the department.*

*Right, of course—*

*We're not... Creative Humanities.*

What's wrong with Creative Humanities?

And was that a threat? It felt like a threat of some kind.

*Rules can be limiting.* Me, trying to be light.

*But useful*, he said. *Parameters. Yardsticks. Touchstones. Tenets...*

Have you swallowed a thesaurus, I thought. A little irritated. But didn't say.

*Conventions.* He was still going. *Guidelines. By which to judge things. Examine them. Compare.*

I don't want to compare myself, I thought again. To anything actually. That's something I'd really like to stop.

*Rules can be limiting,* I countered, *to imagination.*

*This is science.*

Well there's no arguing with that. No point, I mean. Not with Raoul. Who has clearly set his own limits on his own imagination.

Right then. A different tack...

*The thing is I've been reading a lot lately around the idea of feminist glaciology.* Which I had. *And it allows for a much wider view of landscape and the environment. And... ice. Because ice isn't just ice. And we need to look beyond its physical properties. To—*

*Oh god, really?* he interrupted.

*Really...?* What? Really what?

*This is where we are now isn't it?* he declared, I would go so far as to say, sneeringly. *I thought we were just studying the world around us. Scientifically.*

*We are the world around us.* I felt that was fair to point out.

*Well I think that's a little egocentric.*

Me? What a dick.

*Well I guess we're all the main protagonist in our own stories.*

At least, that's what I'm trying to be, I realised it as I said it. And stop seeing other people as the main protagonist. Like you Raoul. Or my mother for instance. For too long she had been the main protagonist in my story. Now, I was trying to make it me.

He didn't know what to say to that, and caught the eye of someone much more important over my shoulder and sidled off to over-enthusiastically greet them.

And I reflected for a moment how that actor that I'd heard, on the radio, had been helped along somewhat. She'd had a writer and a director. And she'd practiced. And rehearsed. A lot probably. Before she fully assumed her role. She didn't just become her overnight.

---------

Halloween—I dressed up. And trick or treated with the children who were visiting.

And Christmas. I loved Christmas. The atmosphere in
the home. The tree and the lights and the carols, which
I helped to organise. And the Secret Santa presents, which
I helped to wrap.

Tom's dad had to work a shift at the last minute, which meant
that I had him for the whole day. So I decided, rather than ask
my neighbour if she could watch him for a while, to take him
with me to the home. It was a whim. Or, on a whim. I didn't
ask Eve if she thought that was all right, which I really should
have, I know. But I think the reason I didn't was because if
I did and she said no, then I wouldn't have been able to. And
I really wanted him to meet Edith.

I'd wanted it for a while.

I'd been dreaming of introducing her to Tom for the first time.
And saying, *Look Edith, here's your grandson. Isn't he great? He loves
to read too. Like you did.*

And in my dream Tom would settle in the corner with his
book, and a companionable silence would ensue. And then
Nurse Myka would come in with tea and biscuits at 3 p.m.
It had started to become a recurring dream. And while I'm
not a trained psychiatrist—obviously—even I knew that
dreams that surface again and again, are doing it for a reason.
Let's not forget all those books by Jung on the shelves.

*So, we're going to see Eve's mother,* I said to Tom. By way of preparation.

*She's older, and she doesn't make a lot of obvious sense. So don't be scared. Are you scared?*

He shook his head.

*I mean you don't have to come with me, if you don't want to. I could just pop in. But I'd rather go in for longer.*

He shrugged.

*Yes?*

He nodded.

*I'm doing it because Eve can't. She's busy. And no one wants to be on their own at Christmas.* Not entirely true. Some people love it. I myself have, so I am proof.

And he looked at me, a little... sceptical. And I wondered what he might have picked up, what with all our chats. But I thought I'd just ignore that. Too tricky to explain. Or worry about. So—

*The nurses might call me Eve. It's so we don't confuse her mum. Strangers aren't good. So if she hears the name Eve it makes it all easier. More kind of bearable. Make sense?*

A half shrug yes.

*Okay then. Shall we go in?*

He nodded. So we went in.

Edith was in her bedroom—which was good. Less people about. For the moment, just Nurse Claire, who was plumping pillows.

*Hello,* I said. *I have someone with me today.*

And Edith looked up—sort of interested maybe. Hard to tell.

*This is Tom... I'm just taking care of him for the day.* This was for the nurse's benefit—but I felt bad saying that.

I leant in to kiss her—*Happy Christmas*—then thought maybe I shouldn't have done that. Not in front of Tom. Being too affectionate with her might be a bit confusing for him. But he didn't seem fazed.

He just sat down on the floor, crossing his legs, and opened his book.

And I gave her a gift from Eve. A small hamper, filled with biscuits and chocolates and fruits. And a scarf from me. Also from 'Eve'.

After opening them up, then eating lunch, then watching Christmas TV, later I went out to get some ice cream from the canteen. A bowl for Edith and one for Tom.

*Are you going to be alright?*

He nodded, not looking up.

*Sure?*

Another nod. Emphatic. So I went.

I saw Terry, when I was on my way back.

*What d'you go for?* he asked, nodding at the silver ice cream bowls, which were freezing my fingers.

*Raspberry ripple. And rum and raisin.*

*Old school. I like it.*

*Want some?* I extended out the bowls, giving him a choice. *I can go get more.*

*No, you're alright. Thanks though. And if I did, it'd be rum and raisin. Just so you know, for next time.* A wink.

*Noted.* I winked back.

When I walked into the room, Tom was sitting much closer
to Edith, and seemed to be reading to her, from his notepad.
Lips moving.

And she had her head cocked, to one side. So she could hear
him better?

He quickly stopped when he saw I'd come in. And started
to eat his ice cream when I handed it to him. His eyes not quite
meeting mine.

Huh. Interesting.

And after they'd finished, both scraping their bowls clean—
which was a little grating, but I let it go—we sat up on the bed
and watched *Meet Me in St Louis*, just the three of us.

And Edith fell in and out of sleep, and whenever she woke she'd
sing along... *have yourself a merry little Christmas...*

---------

At first I was upset, of course. Who wouldn't be!?

But after quite some time of having this interloper in my life—
once I'd calmed down and grown used to the arrangement—
I reflected on it. In my more lucid moments. During these
flashes of insight. And I thought hard about why you acted

in such a way. About the chain of events that led you—my daughter—to take such a decision. I mean would I have wanted to sit with my mother? For days, in and out. I hadn't had to make that call. My mother died in her sleep. Decision made.

And the more time I've spent with my pretend Eve—my adopted daughter—I've actually started to admire what you've done. This unwritten contract we had—that I would care for you til you could care for yourself, and you would care for me when I no longer could—could be torn up. The rules rewritten. You didn't ask to be born. To be burdened with life. With your own existence. And you didn't ask to be burdened with mine.

Was the amount of time you chose to spend (or not spend) with me commensurate with your love? Could it be measured in time spent by my side, watching over me, whilst longing, and waiting, to leave. To go and meet some friends. Socialise. Live well, and enjoy the company of others. The two-way conversations. Or just be. Somewhere else. Just be. Without burden.

The more I've thought about it there's care there, actually, in what you've done. You haven't abandoned me. Or discarded our relationship. Instead you sent me someone else. A better version of yourself, in many ways. A version unencumbered with all the shoulds and have-tos—the Christmases and birthdays of obligation.

The fact you've done what you've done at all is actually proof of your care, and love. An acknowledgement that you understand your failings.

You haven't abandoned me at all. You've done it because you are incapable of loving me or caring for me in the very best way you should. So you got someone in who could. Much like a good parent should know when to step aside. When someone else can service their child's needs better than they can. Hurt them less. Heal their wounds better. Do them less damage.

The more I think about it, now, I actually admire you. A great deal more than I ever have. I feel, finally, you have achieved something. Something worthy of my upbringing.

And this person—I don't actually know her name, let's just call her Eve 2—I have to say, really has been very attentive. She's understood my taste in books for one thing.

And the way she brushes my hair—not like when you're a child, and you're at the hairdressers and they tug away at it, pulling the scalp til you want to cry sometimes. She's been really very gentle. Considerate. I don't feel like I irritate her at all. Not at all. She seems to love spending time with me. Accepting me for who I am. Wholeheartedly.

And the way she's rubbed my feet and hands. With a moisturiser, which smells of something lovely that I can't quite put my finger on. It's been nice. Being touched. You don't realise how important it can be. When you're alone. The simple act of touching. Of skin on skin. How it can change your whole day. The course of it. The feel.

I did have that for a time. Not that you knew. You or Danny. But I had a whole other life. With someone just for me. Maybe I was kinder to her. Than my own children. But she understood me. The other sides of me. And that was just for us. I didn't need anyone else to know. Didn't want them to. But looking back on it, in light of what you've done, maybe you knew the whole time. That I was somewhere else. Maybe you sensed it. Deep down. That a part of me was taken up. Still, I stayed. For you. Because I thought I should. That that was the right thing. I stayed.

But that's another story. You'll find no trace of that. Not in any box in any attic. Or any email thread on an old, discarded laptop. I was careful with my love.

---------

And then after everything had been going so well—aside from the Raoul put down, which I was still processing and dealing with—it felt like everything started to go not so well.

First, the home lost Edith. Which was temporary, but unnerving.

Erin had been cleaning the house down the road. And she was running late, apparently—because she'd had to look after the baby. *Again,* she said, rolling her eyes. So she was a bit flustered.

*You could feel it in the air,* she told me later. There was a palpable sense of panic as soon as she'd walked through the door of the home.

*What's going on?* she asked a nurse she didn't know so well, who was passing reception.

*We can't find her.*

*What do you mean?*

*Mrs Monroe. She's disappeared.*

*What?* This immediately freaked her out. *How can she just disappear?*

*We're looking now.* Not quite answering the question, she noticed. *It'll be fine. It happens.*

She tried calling me, in a panic. *Come on, pick up, pick up.* Not wanting to push anything too official without talking to me first. *For obvious reasons.*

But I didn't answer. My phone was on my desk and I was with a student, who was crying about her grades, so I wasn't paying attention. And she got no answer.

She left me a message—*Can you try me, when you get this.* Her voice, trying to be calm but tinged with alarm. So I thought the time we all knew was approaching had come, and Edith had probably died.

*What's wrong?* I called as soon as I'd listened to it.

*It's your—*

And then Terry walked through the door apparently, with Edith on his arm.

*Oh thank god. She's here.*

*What happened, Erin?* Me, trying to get answers.

*It's okay. I'd better go.*

*Well call me,* I told her, frustrated not to know anymore. *As soon as you leave.*

*I will.*

*Where was she?* she asked Terry. Who nodded behind him, over his shoulder

*In the park?*

*Yes. Sitting with the man who sells coffee. At the entrance.*

Weird.

*What happened?* I demanded. She was back at my flat now.

*Someone had left the sliding doors open,* she explained. *Into the garden. And the gate at the back was open too.*

*I can't believe you weren't there.* That just slipped out of me.

*I was at work,* she said. Immediately defensive.

*This is your work.* I carried on, despite myself.

*I can't be there the whole time... You don't pay me enough,* she joked. Trying to deflate the situation. Probably.

But I didn't laugh.

*That's why she's in a care home, Eve.* She was frowning, more serious now. *It's not my fault I wasn't there. I mean you could have been. If you wanted to be.*

She was right, of course. Maybe I should have been. I mean why was I not seeing her? Really? I didn't even have a good reason. *I'm sorry,* I said, taking a deep breath. My hand on her shoulder for a moment. Trying to de-escalate. *That just really... scared me. What if they'd called the police?*

*I know,* she said, clearly shaken too. Her hand, for a moment, over mine. *I think they were about to.*

We just looked at each other, not saying any more. Not really having a solution. Knowing that neither of us was to blame, as such.

Knowing also, that we both were. In a way.

---------

Then, two deaths in the home. Two other residents, who passed away in quick succession. Pete, who was the life and soul, and Jerry, who was much more of a pain, to be honest, but still.

The mood was sombre. It affected everyone. Edith was particularly jittery. Which was happening with increasing regularity. As the doctors had predicted. But this was more so than usual. Like she knew something was up.

Edith unsettled, meant I was unsettled.

*She's very agitated.* Nurse Claire again. She saw me as soon as I'd come through the front doors.

*Oh really? Why?*

*I don't know. Something just set her off. Nurse Myka's with her.*

I hurried down the hall. To find Nurse Myka outside her room. Washing jelly and cream off her plastic apron.

*She's mad but I can't work out what it was. Normally I can work it out.*

*Have you tried music? That usually calms her, no?*

*I've tried. Not working.* She seemed a bit disgruntled. Annoyed with herself, maybe, for not having the solution. *Why don't you tell her something,* she suggested, taking off her apron and putting on a new one. *Something from the past. A good time. Something she loved.*

I racked my brains. I couldn't think. None of the stories that Eve had told me were that... emotional. It was all those fact things. I couldn't do anything with that. And there were certainly no good time stories, though I'm sure there must have been some.

*Let me go in.*

Edith was up on her feet. Very upset. Terry with her, trying to manage her.

*It's alright, love,* he said. *Nothing to worry about here.*

*No,* she kept saying. Just *no, no. No.* Flailing her arms.

*It's okay,* he kept on, a soothing tone. *Come on now. It's okay.*

But it wasn't. Edith was distraught. It was very upsetting.

*Hey Mum.*

*No. No. No.*

Think, think. Think of a story, Erin. Something good. Think, think. Then—

One suddenly came to me. A memory. One of *mine*. With *my* mum.

Could I...? I thought. Then... what the hell. Why not.

So, I ended up telling that. A story from our past. One of our nicer memories together. One that stuck out. That I often replayed in fact. To myself.

*Hey Mum,* I said, sitting down on a chair nearby. *Remember when we went to Alton Towers?*

*No. No. No.*

*It was a real treat, remember? I'd been begging you for ages to take me.
And you saved up and took me for my birthday. I'd read about it. About
all the rides. And you said we were going to go. And you weren't feeling
so good when the time came around. Looking back on it, we probably
shouldn't have gone. Not really. Not just the two of us. But you knew what
it meant to me. And when you'd booked it you'd been really up. Feeling
good about life. And all its possibilities and adventure. And you were like—*

*We are going to go on every single one of those rides. And we are going
to have FUN.*

She was definitely starting to engage, Edith. A bit quieter now.

*And you were really trying I know. For me. Because it was a present. And I
was excited. But you still had to lie down on the bench and just do nothing.
It was all a bit much. And I said to you, you can make a choice I think.
To feel the good rather than the bad. And you listened, and you made a
choice. And we went on a couple of rides, and they were okay. But then you
had to lie down on a bench again and have even more of a rest. So I just sat
there, next to you. While you closed your eyes, and let the world around
you disappear. The world that was just... too much.*

*Do you remember? Do you?*

She was pretty still now.

*So we could just do that now. Close our eyes and let the world around us
disappear. Until there's nothing but just you and me. And it's all okay.*

Weirdly, she actually really did calm down. Maybe it was just the story—the telling of it, I mean—that caught her imagination. Listening so intently.

I looked up, and Terry had tears in his eyes. And so did Nurse Myka, who had come in behind me. She didn't say anything—unusually for her—she just put her hand on my shoulder for a moment, then moved off.

She was probably thinking, why are you telling *that* story? That's a sad story, not a happy one. But it meant something. And in my experience, something that meant something for one person, often can for another. That's stories for you. They can be powerful things.

But it did make me start to worry. Those deaths. About what would happen when Edith died.

I mean I would quickly be cast aside. Wouldn't I? Eve would have no more use for me. Back to cleaning other people's toilets. Full-time. My gateway into this world of privilege and attention would close. And the no entry sign would go back up.

You are not welcome here. You are an interloper. You don't belong. And you have to leave now.

These people had become my family. Staving off my loneliness. Giving me purpose. A sense of place. Tom was brilliant and gorgeous, and I loved him of course. Of course I did. But his silence was a lot sometimes. And Eve had become such an anchor.

What was I going to do? To make sure this didn't happen?

I ran through all the options in my head, noting them down on the back of an envelope—over a glass of red in the little local wine bar.

I could bribe her. Her brother wouldn't take kindly to knowing that a stranger had been visiting his mother. But what she'd done hadn't been illegal. And maybe what I was doing was? Impersonating another person.

I was being irrational now, giving in to my own panic. Every thought more stupid than the first. As if I'd ever bribe her. Ridiculous. And took a large gulp of wine.

But given I'd started to worry about it so much, I thought it was probably wise to broach the topic.

---------

*What's going to happen when she dies?... I mean I don't want to think about it, really, but—*

*What do you mean?*

*To me?... Sorry that sounds really selfish now I say it, but—*

*No, I...* I trailed off. Having nothing proper to say. Momentarily at a loss for words.

Not because I hadn't thought about it as such. I had. But I certainly hadn't thought about it in a way that was formulated enough to properly discuss it. On all sorts of levels.

And now she'd brought it up, I realised it wasn't the practical side of the arrangement that my head immediately went to, but the... more emotional aspect of it. How much she had come to mean to me. How big a part of my life. Her, and Tom. How much her presence had freed me.

*We'll find you another job,* I said.

---------

Just like that.

A little patronising when you think about it. And not like her. Not consciously anyway. But these things have a way of showing.

That's the gig economy for you. Right there. I mean who does it really benefit? Talk about putting me in my place.

---------

*It's not that easy*, she said. A little upset I think. Understandably, perhaps. I hadn't meant to make her feel like that.

*Well no, I know, but...* unable to articulate what I wanted to say.

*Do you?*

*Of course. I do read the papers, Erin.* Me, a little defensive.

*Right. Of course you do.* Backing down a bit. Knowing, perhaps, that I hadn't meant it to sound the way it did. *Well the thing is I've got a taste now.*

*For care homes?*

*For freedom.*

---------

And then, the worst thing. Potentially.

---------

The thing I hadn't really expected to happen.

---------

*We have a problem.*

*What?*

I stopped trying to get the ink stain out of Tom's shirt where it had leaked through his pocket. This was serious. I could tell by Eve's tone.

*Danny's coming home.*

*What?* Shit.

*For work.*

*What are we going to do?*

*I don't know.*

I ran through the options in my head. None of them brilliant.

*I—you—could be away?*

*No, I can't. Not with my work.*

*Ill?*

*Done that.*

*Lost your phone? Dog ate your homework…?*

She shook her head.

*Did you know this was going to happen?* That came out a bit more accusing than I meant it.

*No.* Defensive. *I don't think he thought he was ever going to see her again. In the flesh. Not really. But I guess she's lasting longer than we thought.*

*Ouch.*

*I didn't mean it like that.*

Didn't she?

*It's just…* she went on to explain. *Sometimes I do wonder if you're actually keeping her alive.*

*What do you mean?*

*Giving her a reason to… keep going.*

Which I loved. The idea that Edith might be sticking around because of me.

*Maybe I did the wrong thing, sending her you.*

No. Don't say that. I'd hate to think that. I want to be the right thing. Not the wrong thing. *I think she just wants to keep going. She's just a keep going sort of person.*

*Anyway, Danny.*

*Couldn't you try just not going in at the same time?* I asked. *Me, I mean.*

*Maybe.*

*Like you want to give them some space. So, he can have some quality time with her.*

*Nice idea. Just not sure that's going to work. He's here for over a week.*

Which meant that I wouldn't be able to go in for over a week. Which felt like a really long time.

---------

*How could you?* Danny was back and I'd had to tell him everything. I'd explored all the options and nothing was going to work. It was just too risky. Him working it out when he was actually at the home. It would humiliate him. And put him on the defensive. And that was the last thing I needed.

How predictable, though—that line... *how could you?*

*How could I?* I said. *Well easily, it turns out.*

*But what were you... thinking?*

Where to start?

*I'm really... shocked, Eve. It's a horrible betrayal.*

*She doesn't know, Danny.*

*But we know. I know.*

Yes.

*I mean who is this person? How did you even meet her? She could be anybody. She could be a...* he faltered.

*What?*

*Psychopath. Deranged. Out for her money.*

*We're not in a Hollywood melodrama. This is just real life. I offered her a job—because she needed one—and she took it.*

*A weird job.*

*But is it? When you really think about it?*

*Yes.*

*Why do you assume the worst? She's actually really nice. Maybe you should meet her.*

*No, I don't think so.*

*Try and... get to know her.*

*I don't want to get to know her. I don't need to get to know her because we're going to have to stop this right now.*

*Why?*

*It's obvious why.*

*But—*

*I should never have left, I knew it.*

*Yes you should.*

*You can't take the responsibility you need to take.*

*This is me taking responsibility.*

He threw me a look then. *A really???!!!* look. That implied he thought entirely the opposite of what I was saying. And that I did too, but just wasn't admitting it.

*Do you want some port?* Me, trying to diffuse the situation.

*Port?* His look incredulous, as if I'd offered him strychnine.

*Yes, you left me with a taste for it. And now it calms me.*

*Fine.*

I went and got the port and poured it into a little glass. One for him. And then one for me.

*Cheers.* I raised my glass.

He didn't reply. Or raise his glass.

*See?* I said, after he finally drank.

*It's good,* he admitted. And took another swig. *But it doesn't mean I'll change my mind.*

Then, after a long moment of thought—

*You know what,* he said, and I knew something was coming... *I think, if you don't see her you think it's not really happening.*

Boom. Gut punch.

And I have to admit—he got me there.

That was going to take a bit of time to process.

*I think,* he continued, *that you just want to remember her as she was. Not as she is. And by not seeing her that's what you can do. Or maybe, that you magically think it's not really going to happen at all. That if you don't go and see her, that she won't die. Either way, I think you're burying your feelings.*

What's wrong with wanting to remember someone as they were? What's wrong with burying feelings? Sometimes it's the only thing that helps. It's there for a reason... forgetting. All this insistence, on... facing things. Leaning in. I don't know. It's good sometimes. Of course. I'm not saying run away. Don't face anything. But sometimes... feeling everything you can is... overrated. Too complicated. Too challenging. Too... conflicting. And not remotely... enjoyable. In the long run. Or the here and now.

That's what I wanted to say.

But I didn't, I said—

*Do you have to say something?*

*Of course.*

*What happens if you don't?*

*Why would I do that?*

*For me,* I shrugged. Being honest.

*But it's the logical thing to do.*

*Maybe. But what if you tried to see the logic of not.*

*What do you mean?*

More port.

*Well, rather than assuming—or confirming—that your own logical path of action is in fact the right one, how about trying to just see it from a different point of view. Change the narrative.*

*Huh.*

He was my brother and I loved him, but it took a while sometimes.

---------

*Why don't I speak to him?* I asked Eve.

*He doesn't want to talk to you.*

*Why?*

*Well he's my brother and I love him,* she said, *but he tends to follow the most obvious path. However he first reacts to something, is how he then continues. Do you see?*

*Sort of. No.*

*He doesn't want to—be like that necessarily. It's just what he does. He's not one for exploring all the options. Quite a useful way to be, in many ways, but still.*

*Maybe this time he'll surprise you.*

*Maybe. I mean he did surprise me by going to Australia.*

*Good surprise? Bad surprise?*

*Good. It was the coming back that's not worked out so well.*

---------

And then he called me. Unexpectedly.

*I've been thinking.*

*Oh? Careful.* Trying to make a joke.

No response. Not even a smirk. I could tell from his voice. And usually, he's got a pretty good sense of humour. Though not when he's stressed. Or caught up in a serious moment of contemplation. I guess this was a bit of both.

*I'll meet her.*

So people can surprise you. The people you think you know.

---------

I was really nervous meeting Danny. Almost more nervous than when I first met Edith. Like I was going on a proper job interview. And the person who was going to be asking me the questions had already decided on the outcome. Rendering my answers, irrelevant.

I asked Eve to tell me everything she could that might be useful. So I didn't say the wrong thing without thinking. So that I could make as good a case as possible for why I was the right person for the job. The only person.

*He can be a bit tricky,* she said.

So can you, I thought. So can we all.

*You get on though, right? You like him?*

*I do, I suppose. When push comes to shove.*

*When push comes to shove?*

*No, I do. A lot actually. I don't know why I'm being negative. Habit.*

Well Danny Monroe. Bring it on. I'm ready for you... ish.

---------

I was nervous, knowing that Danny was with Erin. It made me feel really vulnerable. Like two people were discussing me and I wasn't part of the equation and couldn't put a word in for myself. To account for myself.

I didn't like it. Not one bit. Like my sense of self was slipping away. And I couldn't secure it.

I was all up in my throat—constricted and tight—not down in my stomach, where I needed to be.

So I did some breathing exercises... to calm down. But it didn't really work. Nor did the port. A temporary tactic, I'd started to realise, to life's problems, that was increasingly wearing off.

---------

He'd suggested we meet at the wine bar that I was still going to, near the home. He was visiting Edith, in the afternoon, so it would be convenient.

*Neutral territory*, he said. In his text. As if we were in a war. And I was the... aggressor.

Not the best start.

He was late. Which I assumed was deliberate. Some kind of power thing, maybe. Though I was probably overthinking it, and he was just late. Edith didn't like it when people left. Which meant I had a bit of time to chat to Florence, who worked behind the bar.

She was there part-time, Florence, while studying at the university close by, to be a vet. And I'd rather hoped she wouldn't be in today. Not because I didn't like her. I did. I really liked her. We'd had lots of very interesting chats over the last few months. But I only hoped she wasn't there because she thought I was called Eve and I was a glaciologist. It just sort of slipped out when I was in one day having a glass of wine after seeing Edith. When one of my cleaning jobs was cancelled at the last minute. And before I was due to get Tom from an after-school club. And she'd engaged me in conversation, asking what book I was so engrossed in. And what I was reading was a book about climate change, with an essay in by Eve. I don't know why I did it. It just kind of came out of me. I guess—because I'd only just come from the home—I was sort of still in character. At least that's what I told myself. So I filled her in about the topic and said that one of the essays was mine. Which she'd thought was very cool. Being as how she cared so much about the environment, and what we were actually going to do about it.

*Hey,* she said, when I walked in. *What's going on in the ice world?*

So actually it was good he was late, I realised. To get this chat out the way.

*Not much.*

She was a bit surprised by that. Usually I engaged a lot more, given I'd got to know quite a lot now, about glaciology.

*What can I get you? The usual?*

*I'm meeting someone, actually. So, I'll wait.*

*Oh, who—*

*Oh, here he is.*

I saw him walking through the door, Danny, and recognised him instantly, from his pictures. I'd spent so much time looking at them, while Edith dozed off, it was strange seeing him in real life.

*Danny.* I really hoped he wouldn't say my name.

*Hello.*

*Shall we...* I urged him towards a table at the back, away from Florence and the bar.

*What would you like?*

*I'll get them,* he said.

*It's okay. I'd like to.*

He hesitated. Maybe not wanting to be indebted to me. For anything.

*Just a coffee then,* as he turned away and sat.

*Can we have two coffees please.* Me to Florence. Though at this point I actually really wanted wine, I felt it might not be the best look.

*Sure,* she nodded.

*So...* he said, as I sat down.

*Thanks for meeting with me.* Thanks for meeting with me? I'd never said anything like that in my entire life.

*It seemed to make sense,* he said. *Given the... circumstances.*

*Of course.*

...

*So don't you think it's a bit... odd. What you're doing?*

*Not really.*

*Right. Okay.* Disbelieving.

*Well I suppose I did, at first.*

*At first?*

*Yes. I mean it wasn't like I was looking for it. Obviously. This job.*
But Eve—I lowered my voice, aware of Florence by the coffee
machine staring/not staring. *Eve suggested it so...*

*Yes she said.*

*Once she had and once I thought about it, I could see how it made sense.*

*So what do you get out of it?*

*A salary,* I joked. Sort of. *And... satisfaction.*

*Shouldn't you be looking after your own mother?*

*She's dead.*

*Oh. I'm sorry.* He did look very... contrite, I think you'd say is the word. *My sister didn't tell me that.*

*Here you go.* This was Florence.

*Thanks.*

*Thanks.*

*Okay then. Let me know if you need anything else.*

We both nodded.

*We will.*

And then there was silence, as she walked away, clearly intrigued because I'd never been in here with anyone before and she probably thought we were on a date.

*But if she could have had someone to look after her,* I resumed the conversation. *Who was devoted to her... needs. That would have made me happy.*

*Someone like you?*

*Yes.*

*That's ironic.*

*A different version of me. Superior, I guess.*

*So I should be looking for a different, more superior version of you for my mother?*

*Funny.*

*I can be, actually. I imagine Eve didn't tell you that.*

I think I went red then. I could feel myself flushing.

*Well I imagine you have discussed me.*

*A little.*

*I won't ask.*

*Point is,* I said. *It seems I can be the things that Eve can't.*

*Point is, shouldn't she at least try to be?*

*Seems like maybe she's done with trying.*

He didn't say anything to that.

*I really do... care for her, you know.*

*Eve?*

*Edith.*

*You don't know her.*

*I feel like I do. How well do you? Now?* Pushing my luck there, I'll grant you.

*Better than you.*

*Yes. But you left.*

*Not sure you're fighting your corner very well here, Erin.*

Yeah, this really wasn't going so well.

*And I suppose, the thing is, that she's sort of a different person, isn't she? Than she was. Edith, I mean.*

I didn't really want to get into all the ways that Eve was now being a different person. I felt that was between them.

*Yes,* he said, clearly emotional. *I suppose she is... and they do seem to really, really like you,* he added.

*Who?* I asked, confused.

*Everyone. In the home. How you are with her. Apparently, and I say this without irony, you are the model child.*

That caught me off guard. For a moment, I felt like my heart was going to burst. Just knowing that, I—

*But you do know, she's not actually your mother, right?*

*Yes, of course, I—*

*Hey Eve, can I get you anything else?* Florence again. Back to see if this was indeed, as she suspected, a date.

I held my breath, aware of how extremely odd Danny might find this. The fact that a student working in a bar was calling me by his sister's name. Thinking it might tip him back over the edge when we were now, quite out of the blue, doing really pretty well.

*Yes, Eve,* said Danny, eyes dancing. Thoroughly enjoying the moment. *Want anything else?*

Phew.

He could be fun.

---------

We had a final night before he left, Danny and I.

*Are you looking forward to getting back?*

*I am. People treat us differently there.*

*Is that why you went?*

*I suppose, in part. We were stuck in such a rut here. And I didn't know how to get out of it, without just starting fresh. Somewhere else. Where people don't know you. A bit like starting a new job as a non-smoker. When before you've been a twenty-a-day. But no one knows that in the new place so they don't even associate you with smoking.*

*Or define you by it?*

*Exactly.*

*Plus, it means it's easier to then keep up the no smoking.*

*Good point.*

...

*You know,* he said next. *It's highly likely that I won't see her again. More than.*

*You thought that before.*

*I did. But seeing her now, there's really very few properties left. So if you're going to see her again... at all. Well.* He let the unsaid words hang there, not being said.

*You know...* I said. Not sure if I was saying this for him. Or myself. Or both... *there's a saying in McMurdo, for the people who are leaving. You say your goodbyes, to all the people you've lived with for so long. Co-existed with. Been irritated by. Maybe fancied a little. Or been awed by. Or dismissive of. Learnt from. Affected. You say your goodbyes, to all these people you'll probably never see again, even though you all swear you will. Like the last day of school. Or some sort of camp. And you head for the plane. Thinking about how you're going to adjust to being back in the real world. The people you haven't seen for ages. How you have probably really changed and they probably really haven't. And then it's cancelled, because of weather. As per. And you go back and spend more time with these people. Maybe a day or two, depending. Could even be a week. Til the next plane. And then you do it all again. The goodbyes.*

*They are called the Ungone.*

---------

*I think he's surprised, Danny,* Eve said. It was around a week later.

*About?*

*That this whole thing has actually worked so well. How much it suits him, this situation. I think he's much happier, really. Knowing you've been there with her. Are there with her. Rather than me.*

We were out for a bowl of something, near her flat. Her treat, she said. To celebrate our success. That everything was back to normal.

*Jealous?* I asked. Jokingly. But interested to know.

*Of someone I've asked to be me?*

*I guess.*

*Sometimes. Probably.*

I hadn't expected that.

*But that's on me.*

Fair enough.

*It's made me realise how much I've been defining my relationship to him through our relationship to her. Danny via Edith. And that it doesn't have to be that way.*

*That's good, isn't it?*

*Yes.* She put some more dressing on the salad we were sharing, and tossed it around a bit. *Plus, he's chipping in.*

*Oh. That's generous.*

*That's guilt.*

*Maybe I should ask for a pay rise,* I said, as she put some on my little side plate.

*I'd say. It's good to know what you're worth.*

We ate for a moment, then... something I often wondered about, and had never asked—

*Why did your mother call you Eve?*

*I don't know,* she shrugged.

*Didn't she say?*

*No. You could always ask her.*

*Funny.*

*I'm learning.*

*You are.*

*It's true though. Why burden me? With this name. Eve. It's connotations. Almost like she expected me to be behave like an Eve. Set me up. In fact,* she said, putting down her fork. *The more I think about it, it's quite a thing to even decide to call someone Eve. Not even passive aggressive, just downright aggressive.*

Interesting. She'd never talked this... emotionally about Edith before. I realised I must have hit a nerve of some kind.

*Maybe what I need to do is just... change it.*

*You know,* I ventured, putting down my fork. *I've been thinking...*

*Careful.*

*That maybe you've been spending so much time trying on other versions of yourself, that you have absolutely no idea who you are anymore.*

A frown, as she started to think about that.

*That actually what you've been doing is moving further and further away from yourself.*

*Or further and further towards.*

*That actually you're moving further and further away from yourself, when actually yourself is pretty great.*

Silence. No words from her at that.

*And I say that as someone who's been being you for months.*

*Not the real me.* Tone light-hearted. Not matching the look
on her face.

*But you do know that, don't you?*

Again. No words.

*I just feel sometimes that maybe you don't. That you're trying to be this
unattainable thing. Rather than who you actually are. You're pretty hard
on yourself, you know.*

*Am I?*

*I'd say.*

*Aren't you? Hard on yourself? Isn't everybody?*

*Not everybody. I reckon some people could probably do with being a bit
more hard on themselves. But yes, now you mention it, I think I have
been. Just in a different way. I've realised that now. Because of Edith.
Even though she's not actually my mother,* I said, Danny's words
ringing in my head. *It's weird,* I confided. *How much I still want
her to care.*

She nodded. *Well that I get.*

*Anyway,* I said, scooping up the last of my spaghetti sauce,
*I just think you need to trust that who you are is pretty great.* Thinking…
I'll just leave that one there. To percolate.

*Well, then, I'll bear that in mind.*

---------

And I did. Because Erin is very clever. And thinking about it,
in this case, probably right.

---------

Where does a story end? Who's in control?

I'd like to be, I've decided. In control of mine.

To choose my own ending. The how and the when.

So now,

I think,

I'm just going to go.

I think I've had enough, of being Edith. I've worn out her use.

For me, and everyone else.

I think that everyone needs to move on.

And if I go, they can do that.

To what, I don't know.

But on they can go. With their own stories.

And so can I.

Just.

Go.

I really want to now.

Tonight. When everyone's left. And I'm alone.

Somewhere... else.

---------

I was getting ready to leave this afternoon, when Edith said
something to me that she'd never said before, in all my months

of coming. She just turned, after I'd leant down to gently kiss her forehead and swung my bag up onto my shoulder (the bag which Eve had given me) and said—

*I love you.*

I froze. Stopped in my tracks. Surprised. And overcome. Not sure if I'd heard right at first, but knowing that I had. Just staring down at her.

And her eyes met mine—held them for a long time—and then she nodded.

And I thought, she does know. She does know, and she wants me here. She wants me here, and this is where I should be.

And then the veil came back down.

I walked down the corridor, welling up...

Passing Terry. Who frowned.

*Everything all right?*

*Yes,* I nodded. Meaning—I don't know. But I think so.

*Sorry, silly question,* he said. *Sometimes, these things just get to you, don't they?*

*Yes, that's it.*

*See you tomorrow?*

*Tomorrow.*

*Lovely.* He grinned. *Cappuccino a-go-go. Once you've fixed the machine.*

*Deal.*

*Chin up then.*

*It's okay,* I said, tilting my chin up with my own finger. *I'm okay, see? Really, I am. More than.*

*Grand.*

As I walked through the car park, I dialled—

---------

I was cleaning the kitchen when the phone rang, excited to tell Erin my news. That I'd been approached by a professor in the philosophy department who'd heard my paper at the conference—the one that Raoul was so disparaging of—and wanted to talk about funding a secondment. Because he thought it was *cutting edge.* And *of the moment.* And *part of the zeitgeist.* And that Raoul, needless to say, was furious. Which I knew would please her. And that I also knew I'd never have even got to this point without her.

And I was enjoying making the surfaces as spotless as I could— just the way she liked it. Giving them the focus and attention she would have given them herself. As she does to everything that matters.

*How is she?* The first question I always had, when I answered.

*She's fine. Good.*

*Good. So what's going on?*

*Nothing. I just sat with her, really. We just sat.*

*That sounds nice.*

*It was.* Then, *Can I... ask you something?* she asked, a little hesitant. A little doubt in her voice.

*Of course.* I stopped what I was doing.

*Why did you pick me? Way back then. When we first met. Why did you pick me?*

I thought about it for a moment, remembering the way she clutched that coat to her, and the weight of her. The hidden depths.

*You seemed,* I said, *like you were someone who would understand. Like someone who would care. And not judge.*

A sharp intake of breath, down the phone, and then a silence. Unusual for her. And I sensed she might be crying.

*Fancy coming over for a glass of something?*

*Yeah,* she said. *Love to. I'll have to bring Tom.*

*Do,* I replied. *I'd like that.*

I was about to ring off, when—

*I searched it online by the way.*

*What?* I asked. Confused.

*Your name. Eve. You know it means life?*

*Does it?*

*Yes, I looked it up.*

*Huh.*

*She was giving you a nice name. Not a bad one. Just saying.*

And then she was gone.

Huh.

Isn't it weird, I thought, as I imagined her picking Tom up from school and making her way over to my flat, checking there was enough wine cold, even though I knew there was. How we're all just... sitters.

Sitting in.

Either we're sitting in for someone else, or sitting in for ourselves. So many different versions we could be, or want to be, or think we can't be. Holding ourselves up constantly, against ourselves. Our best selves. Our worst selves. Selves. Selves. Selves. Everywhere. Happy. Sad. Trying. Failing. Falling. Being. Trying to be. Not being able to just BE. Becoming and becoming and becoming and becoming.

Exhausting.

Pointless even.

But still we go on. Don't we?

Finding our own ways.

# Acknowledgements

Many thanks to Nina, Will, Craig and Sonny at Rough Trade
Books for generally being brilliant, both as publishers and
people. To Vikki and Ian, for reading, re-reading and discussing.
To Sophie and Sarah for great advice and support; to Sally
too, during all the swims. To Chrissy and everyone at
BookBar, for invaluable chats and caring so much about
books, and the people that read them. And to my agent
Alice, for buckets of enthusiasm and so completely getting it.

ROUGH TRADE BOOKS

**roughtradebooks.com**

9 781914 236587

# Hannah Patterson

Hannah Patterson is a London-based writer for stage and screen. Her plays include *MUCH*, *Giving*, *Platinum*, *Eden* and *Playing With Grown Ups*, which was nominated for an Off West End Award for Best New Play. She is winner of The Athena List for screenwriting and producer of the award-winning documentary *Shelter in Place*. She has written and spoken about film and culture for The Guardian, Time Out, Sight & Sound and Radio 4, and is editor of the acclaimed essay collection *Poetic Visions of America: The Cinema of Terence Malick*. *Ungone* is her first novel.